The Christmas Sea Sleigh

© SANNE ROTHMAN

'Twas the night before Christmas and all through their Christmas vows,

every marvelous creature's heart was stirring as they merrily bowed

xoxo The Author

WHAT WOULD HAPPEN IF YOU CAUGHT A
RAIN DROP,
TEARDROP,
AND DEWDROP?

THE SPRINKLES OF WATER WILL
SPLASH,
SPARKLE,
AND SNOWBALL
INTO A MAGICAL TICKET TO ~

Hop Aboard

THE CHRISTMAS SEA SLEIGH
TO SEE WHAT YOU SPOT !

DASHING THROUGH THE SNOW OR IN THE WINTRY SKY,
SLEIGHS PULLED BY HORSES, DOGS, OR REINDEER MIGHT CATCH YOUR EYE.
BUT DID YOU KNOW, THERE IS ANOTHER SLEIGH CARRIED BY
OCEAN ANIMALS THAT KNOW HOW TO SWIM AND FLY ?

IT'S THE CHRISTMAS SEA SLEIGH AND
IT'S FLOWN BY FANTASTIC SEA CREATURES.
THEY COLLECT THE STORIES IN EACH RAIN DROP, TEARDROP
AND DEWDROP TO SHARE WITH JOYMAKER SEEKERS.

THE CHRISTMAS SEA SLEIGH IS FILLED WITH MORE THAN CANDIES
AND COOKIES FROM BAKERS.
IT'S OVERFLOWING WITH MORE THAN PRESENTS FROM TOYMAKERS.
ITS SEAT IS SAVED FOR THE BEST GIFT OF ALL ~
THE JOYMAKERS!

JOYMAKERS DELIVER A CHRISTMASTIME GIFT ON THIS MARVELOUS RIDE.
IT'S A GIFT THAT GUARDS THE GOOD EVERY DAY AND EVERY NIGHT:
WHEN YOU PRACTICE CHEER AND JOY FAR AND WIDE.
IT LEADS YOU TO A TREASURE TROVE ~
THE COURAGE TO CONQUER ANY TIDE!

Soar Along with

NARWHAL

OTTER

BLUE WHALE

SEAHORSE

PUFFIN

and BABY SEAL

AND HOLD FAST TO THE CHRISTMAS SEA SLEIGH WHEEL,
IN A CHRISTMAS STORY THAT ONLY YOU CAN MAKE REAL.

ABOVE SNOWY MOUNTAIN TOPS AND ACROSS
THE SEVEN SEAS THEY'LL BE RIDING
ON A VOYAGE TO BRING GLAD TIDINGS.
CAN YOU SPOT THEIR MERRY FINS FLAPPING AND
JOLLY TAILS JINGLING SO KINDLY ?

I SWIM IN OPEN WATERS AROUND ICE CHUNKS THAT ARE NOT SMALL.

I CAN SHOW YOU HOW TO Uplift SOMEONE WHEN THEY FALL.

First, smile

THEN

SAY TO THEM THEY ARE NOT ALONE ~ NOT EVER AT ALL

I'M FURRY, CINNAMON BABY OTTER.

I LIKE TO FLOAT, PADDLE, AND SLIDE IN THE WATER.
I CAN SHOW YOU HOW TO **Comfort** SOMEONE IF THEY TOTTER.

First, give them a hug
THEN
SQUEEZE EVEN HARDER AS YOU HELP THEM FOCUS ON WHAT MATTERS.

I'M MIGHTY, BLUE BABY WHALE.

I ROLL AND TURN IN THE OCEAN SO THE SUN CAN SEE THE
GRAY DOTS DELICATELY PAINTED ON MY FINS AND TAIL.
I CAN SHOW YOU HOW TO BE **Wise and Strong** IF YOU FEEL FRAIL

First, think of a good deed

THEN

DO IT BEFORE YOU GO TO SLEEP AND YOU WILL PAVE A FRUITFUL TRAIL

I'M MINIATURE, TWIRLY TAIL BABY SEAHORSE.

I PLAY HIDE-AND-SEEK IN CORAL REEFS AND GRASS SEA BEDS
AND I CHANGE COLORS OF COURSE.
I CAN SHOW YOU HOW TO Love EVEN WHEN THE
GROUCHIES TRY TO STOP YOU IN FORCE.

First, look at a person that
you would not trade for the whole wide world
THEN
BE THANKFUL THAT YOU ARE THEIRS AND THEY ARE YOURS.

I USE MY SHORT WINGS TO DIVE OFF COASTAL CLIFFS AND
INTO THE DEEP BLUE FOR A SPIN.
I CAN SHOW YOU HOW TO BREAK THROUGH DARKNESS AND
Capture Brightness ANYWHERE YOU'VE BEEN.

First, hold your hands or the hand of a friend
THEN

LOOK UP TO SEE THAT THE TWINKLE IN THE NIGHT CANNOT BE HIDDEN.

IT SHINES ON YOU ALWAYS, EVEN THEN.

I'M SNUGGLY BABY SEAL

I WRIGGLE ON MY BELLY TO TAKE A DIP IN THE SEA
AND USE MY FLIPPERS TO CARTWHEEL.

I CAN SHOW YOU HOW TO BE AT Peace EVEN
WHEN YOUR HEART SEEMS TO BE CARRYING A LOAD OF STEEL.

First, slowly breathe in and slowly breathe out

THEN

WHISPER THAT WE CAN CLEAR AWAY TROUBLES WHEN IT'S

CALM THAT STEERS HOW WE THINK AND FEEL.

Who ~

TUGS FREE THE LIGHT FROM THE DEEPEST FRAY EVEN ON BLUSTERY DAYS ?

ROARS WITH THE MAJESTIC SEA ANIMALS AS THEY JUMP TO HUG THE LIGHT PEEKING THROUGH THE DEW, TEARS, AND RAIN ?

SAILS UNDER THE SKY AND OCEAN REMEMBERING TO BE FAITHFUL IN THE SMALL THINGS ?

CELEBRATES THIS COURAGE WITH A DRUMMING IN THEIR HEART BECAUSE IT'S HOW THEY WILL RISE OVER THE RUSHING WAVES ?

Joymakers ~
Wild & Brave!

from Sunrise to Sunset,

NARWHAL UPLIFTS

OTTER COMFORTS

BLUE WHALE IS WISE AND STRONG

SEAHORSE LOVES

PUFFIN CHASES BRIGHTNESS

BABY SEAL SEEKS PEACE

and from Starfish to Starlight

YOU CAN ALSO DO THESE!

ONCE YOU TRY, YOU WILL SEE THIS GIFT
FOR THE COURAGE THAT IT IS
AND THAT YOU ARE A JOYMAKER FULL OF
HOPEFULNESS,
SWEETER THAN THE GINGERBREAD HOUSE,
MORE GLEEFUL THAN ELF,
AND LOUDER THAN THE SILVER BELLS.

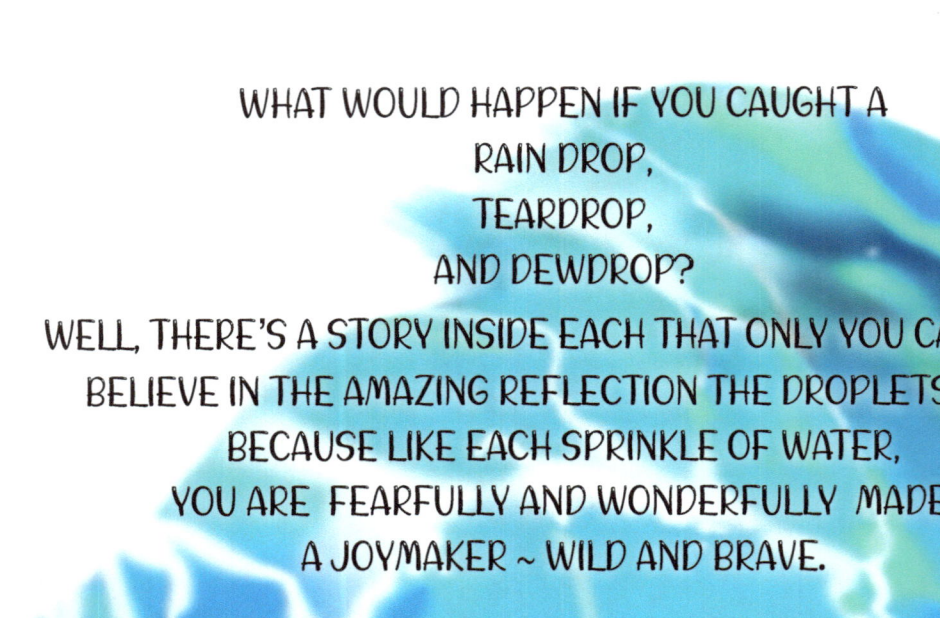

WHAT WOULD HAPPEN IF YOU CAUGHT A
RAIN DROP,
TEARDROP,
AND DEWDROP?

WELL, THERE'S A STORY INSIDE EACH THAT ONLY YOU CAN SPOT.
BELIEVE IN THE AMAZING REFLECTION THE DROPLETS GIVE.
BECAUSE LIKE EACH SPRINKLE OF WATER,
YOU ARE FEARFULLY AND WONDERFULLY MADE,
A JOYMAKER ~ WILD AND BRAVE.

Onward in and out of the water,

THE CHRISTMAS SEA SLEIGH BRINGS COURAGE FOR THE MARVELOUS RIDE TO THE LIONHEARTED ~ EVERY SON AND EVERY DAUGHTER!

THE CHRISTMAS SEA SLEIGH JOYMAKER CARDS

With an adult, cut out the double-sided cards.

NARWHAL

Enjoy Joymaker!

SEAL NARWHAL SEAHORSE OTTER WHALE

Place your cards anywhere!

Take on the go.

NARWHAL

UPLIFTS

TO ENCOURAGE JOY AND BRING CHEER TO
SOMEONE'S SPIRIT AND MOOD

OTTER

COMFORTS

TO SOOTHE, REASSURE AND PROVIDE
EASE TO SOMEONE WHO IS HURT

WHALE

WISE and STRONG

**THOUGHTFUL AND UNDETERRED TO
GAIN AND UNDERSTAND INFORMATION
BEFORE MAKING A JUDGEMENT**

SEAHORSE

LOVES

HAPPY DEVOTION TO SOMEONE CLOSE TO YOU OR SOMETHING YOU ENJOY A LOT; PLANTING, SPORTS, DRAWING, MUSIC, FOOD, PETS...

PUFFIN

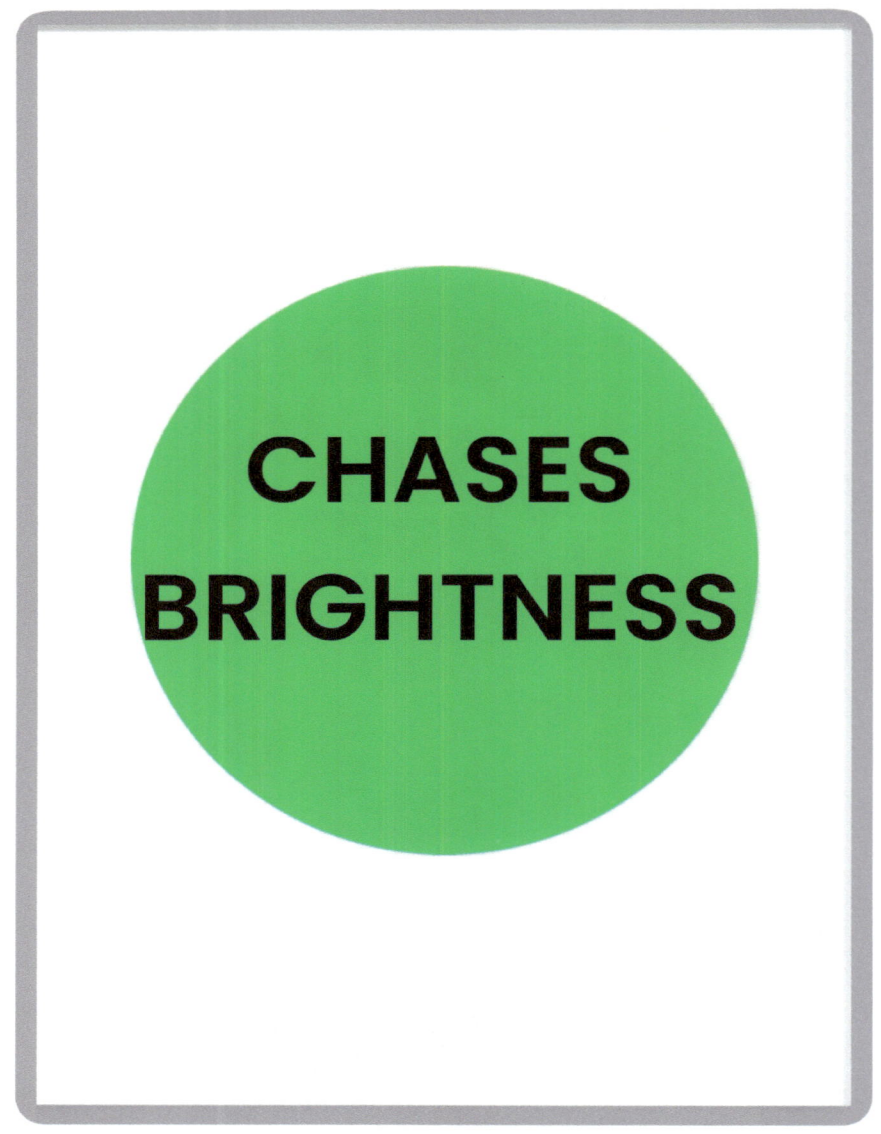

CHASES BRIGHTNESS

CHOOSING TO SHARE JOY AND SEE THE MARVEL
EVEN ON BLUSTERY DAYS, SO THAT NO DAY WILL BE
LOST TO HOLLOW OR NEGATIVE THOUGHTS

SEAL

CHOOSING CALM
TO FIND RESOLUTION TO TROUBLES

Instagram
@ReadersMakeThinkers

More magic of reading from the Author

The Scottie series

The Little Chef series

What's Inside the Christmas Tree

For when they read, they Defeat Giants!

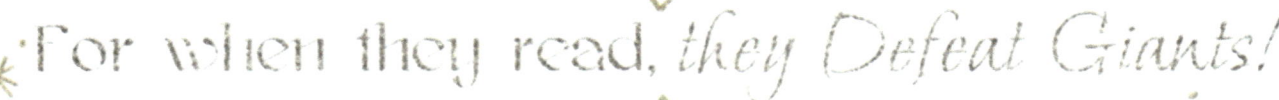

www.ingramcontent.com/pod-product-compliance
Lightning Source LLC
Chambersburg PA
CBHW041545240626
47164CB00003B/139